# A Magic Merry Christmas!

### Concept, Story, and Pictures by
## Amye Rosenberg

GROSSET & DUNLAP

It was a week before Christmas and Queen Josephine's palace was a very merry and busy place. The cooks were busy baking batches of buttery Christmas cookies. The servants were busy decorating the halls with holly.

And the palace children were busy polishing all the ornaments until they sparkled like jewels.

"Now all we need is a very special tree to hang them on," declared the queen.

So Queen Josephine, the servants, and the children all marched off to the forest to find the perfect Christmas tree. Soon the children spotted a stout green fir.

"That's it!" they squealed. "The perfect tree!"

The royal woodcutters chopped and sawed and chopped and sawed. Finally, down came the tree with a huge CRASH!

"Hooray!" cheered the children, jumping for joy in the snow.

But someone in the forest was not happy at all. Deep underground, among the tree roots, lived Malice—a grumpy old wizard if ever there was one. Malice did not like the cold winter, so he slept until spring. The noise above had awakened him, and he was furious.

"How dare you disturb my winter sleep!" he roared.

"We were only cutting down our Christmas tree," replied the queen.

"Christmas tree—phooey!" spat Malice, and he pointed his stick at the beautiful fir.

POOF! The tree disappeared!

"Maybe now I can get some sleep!" grumbled Malice. "And I'm warning you! Don't even try to get another tree, or I'll make it disappear quicker than you can say 'Santa Claus!'"

Then POOF! He disappeared, too.

The children were horrified. How could they have Christmas without their tree?

Queen Josephine was determined to get her tree back. "I know!" she said. "We'll find another wizard to bring our tree back to us!"
So she issued a royal proclamation:

WIZARD WANTED TO FIND MISSING CHRISTMAS TREE.
BIG MAGIC A MUST!

But since Christmas was so close, wizards were in short supply. Two days passed and not a single one could be found.

Things were getting desperate when a scrawny figure appeared at the palace. He wore a wizard's robe and a patched, pointed hat.

"Sir Botchit at your service," he announced, bowing politely.

"Botchit! Now that's an odd name for a wizard," laughed Queen Josephine.

"Well, it's been years since I got a spell right," admitted the wizard. "But if you'll give me the chance, I'll do my best to get back your Christmas tree."

"You're our only chance to have Christmas," said the queen. "When can you start?"

Sir Botchit got to work right away. First he tried to make the water in the royal fountain turn into lemonade. But it just turned into green goo. No one would touch it, let alone drink it!

Then he tried to change the cook's spoon into a candy cane. But he changed the cook, instead!

Finally, he sprinkled a pair of stockings with some magic dust, hoping to make them dance. Up they sprang and danced on a tabletop. Even the wizard was dazzled.

But then, to everyone's dismay, the stockings leapt to the floor and ran out the door. Sir Botchit dashed after them, waving his wand frantically.

"Stop those stockings!" he hollered.

But it was no use. The runaway stockings bolted into the palace kitchen. They crunched over cookies, trampled a cherry pie, and splashed merrily through a bowl of chocolate cake batter.

Finally, they came to rest in the Christmas punch.

"I'm sorry, Your Majesty!" cried Sir Botchit. "I botched it again!"

"Excuse me, Sir Botchit," said a small child tugging at his sleeve, "but I think your wand is upside down."

Sir Botchit looked at his wand. Indeed it *was* upside down!

He turned his wand the other way around. "I am going to try again," said Sir Botchit.

He tapped his wand, right side up. Suddenly, the room was filled with bouncy bubbles, red and green just for Christmas. The children shrieked with glee and tried to catch them. Queen Josephine clapped her hands.

"I did it!" exclaimed Sir Botchit. "I made bubbles appear! Now I can make your tree appear!"

With that, Sir Botchit waved his wand, right side up, and recited a special spell:

BRING US PEACE AND CHRISTMAS GLEE.
BRING US BACK OUR CHRISTMAS TREE!

POOF! The tree stood magnificently before them. Everyone cheered.

Suddenly the branches of the tree rustled. Something thumped to the floor. It was Malice, the grumpy wizard!

"I warned you not to mess with my magic!" he raged. And he lifted his stick.

But Sir Botchit was ready with some magic of his own. And this time he didn't even need his wand.

"Welcome, Malice. Welcome to the palace!" said Sir Botchit. "You have arrived just in time to help us trim the tree!"

Malice stopped right in the middle of his spell. No one had ever been nice to him before.

"Come join us!" said Queen Josephine. "Here's an ornament for you to put on."

"Put on?" wondered Malice, for this was all new to him. He did not know what to do with the shiny ornament. So he hung it at the end of his nightcap. He looked so funny that everyone laughed.